The Cat Next Door

by Betty Ren Wright

illustrated by Gail Owens

Holiday House / New York

For Renée and her Great-Grandma

Library of Congress Cataloging-in-Publication Data
Wright, Betty Ren.
The cat next door / by Betty Ren Wright : illustrations by Gail
Owens.
p. cm.
Summary: After Grandma dies the annual visit to her summer cabin
is not the same but the cat next door remembers how things used to
be and cheers a grieving grandchild.
ISBN 0-8234-0896-5
[1. Cats—Fiction. 2. Grief—Fiction.] I. Owens, Gail, ill.
II. Title.
PZ7.W933Cat 1991   90-29080   CIP   AC
[E]—dc20

Last summer our vacation started when we drove through a dark tree-tunnel and out into the sunshine. "Look!" I shouted. "There's Grandpa's cabin. There's good old Gabe."

The big dog Gabe lay on the back porch. He stood up slowly, with his tail flip-flopping.

My mother said, "Gabe is smiling."

Grandpa and Grandma came out on the porch. We hugged and laughed. Everybody laughed—Grandma and Grandpa and my mother and my father and me. Grandma laughed most of all.

When the grown-ups went inside, I ran around the cabin, past the swing, past the orange flowers that curved like a waterfall over the path. I raced down to the lake and out onto the dock.

I lay on the sun-warm wood and listened to the gulls call *Hello, hello again* from way up in the sky. I peeked between the boards to see the water underneath me.

Swip, swip, it whispered. *Hello again.*

Then Grandma came out on the dock. "I knew I'd find you here," she said.

"I'm waiting for you-know-who," I told her. "Maybe she won't come this year."

Grandma sat down beside me. "She might have lots of things to do on such a splendiferous day, but she'll come if she can. Anyway, you know she'll love you forever and ever."

I lay very still, hoping. Soon I heard a soft sound. It was a tiny, whiny voice. Closer and closer it came. I pretended not to hear.

"You-know-who is coming," Grandma whispered.

"Meow," the voice whined, right in my ear. Something poked me with its nose. Whiskers tickled my chin.

"Meow," said The Cat Next Door. *Where've you been all year, you silly girl?*

The Cat Next Door never said hello to anyone but me. Each morning of my vacation she came out on the dock. She let me rub her stomach. She watched my toes wiggle in the water. When I jumped off the end of the dock with a loud splash, she scooted away, complaining to herself in her tiny, whiny way.

Last summer I learned to swim in the lake. I let Grandma ride on my crocodile raft, and once she fell off. Sometimes she made cookies and lemonade. We had a picnic at the end of the dock.

Every evening we went for a boat ride after supper. Grandpa ran the motor, and I sat with Grandma up in front. We watched for duck babies along the shore. We watched the gulls glide up and down, riding a roller coaster made of air.

Every morning I said, "I wish this day could last forever."

"I do, too," Grandma said. "And it *will* last forever, because that's how long we're going to remember it."

This summer I didn't want to go to the cabin.

"Grandma won't be there," I said. "Nothing will be the same."

My mother looked sad. "You're right," she said. "It will be different this year. But we must go to keep Grandpa company for a while. He's very lonesome."

One morning we drove through the dark tree-tunnel and into the sunshine, just the way we did last summer. The cabin was there, and Gabe was lying on the back porch. He lifted his head, and he wagged his tail once or twice, but he didn't get up.

"The poor old fellow's losing his pep," my father said. I thought, *Gabe is going to die pretty soon, like Grandma did.*

Grandpa came out on the porch by himself. We hugged, but
we didn't laugh the way we did last summer.

Afterward, I walked around the side of the cabin, past the swing and the orange flowers. I looked at the shining silver lake. Gulls rode the waves out in the middle, bobbing like my bathtub toys. I wished Grandma could see them.

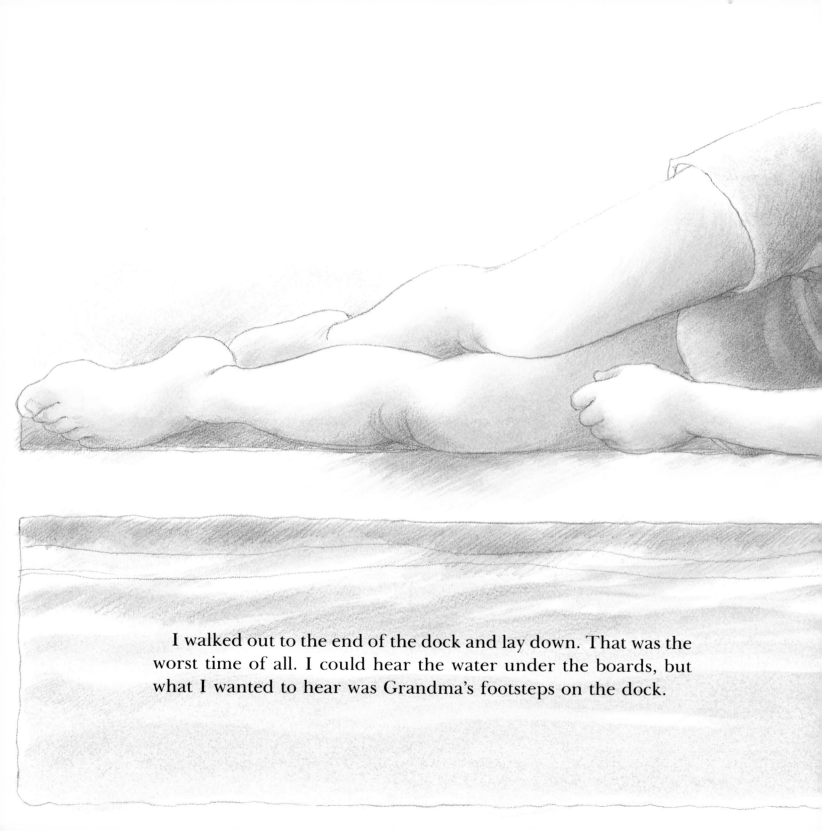

I walked out to the end of the dock and lay down. That was the worst time of all. I could hear the water under the boards, but what I wanted to hear was Grandma's footsteps on the dock.

What I wanted was to hear her call, "How about a sugar cookie, sugar?" I listened hard, trying to make it happen, but the only sound was the *swip, swip* of the water.

I began to cry.

Then I heard something else—a tiny, whiny voice, calling from a long way off. It came closer and closer. I lay very still with my eyes shut tight, pretending not to hear.

Something poked me with its nose. Whiskers tickled my chin. "Meow," the whiny voice said. *Where've you been, you silly girl?*

I opened my eyes and looked at The
Cat Next Door. Then I sat up and
stared. Sitting a little way behind her
were two kittens. One looked just like
The Cat Next Door. The other one
didn't.

I put out my fingers, and the kittens came right up to me. One of them crawled into my lap. The other one tried to bite my big toe. I forgot to feel sad.

Surprised you, didn't I? meowed The Cat Next Door.

The kittens started talking in their tiny, whiny voices. They said, *Where've you been, you silly girl?*

I laughed out loud. It seemed as if I could hear Grandma laughing, too. It seemed as if we were all there, at the end of the dock, together.

"Grandma can't come," I said. "But it's okay. She would love your splendiferous surprise, and so do I. Just remember that she'll love you forever and ever."

"I'll remember," said The Cat Next Door.

Then, for Grandma and for me, I said *hello, hello* to the kittens for the very first time.